Gracem

* 2 2 9 2 4 *

Killer Clone

KT-493-936

Killer Clone

by

Steve Barlow

and

Steve Skidmore

Illustrated by Dylan Gibson

First published in 2009 in Great Britain by
Barrington Stoke Ltd
18 Walker Street, Edinburgh, EH3 7LP

www.barringtonstoke.co.uk

Copyright © 2009 Steve Barlow and Steve Skidmore
Illustrations ©Dylan Gibson

The moral right of the author has been asserted in
accordance with the Copyright, Designs and
Patents Act 1988

ISBN: 978-1-84299-692-8

Printed in Great Britain by Bell & Bain Ltd

Contents

Intro

Every living thing is made out of cells. You are made of billions of them. When human beings are born normally, they take cells from their father and from their mother.

But a clone is a copy of one person and is exactly the same as that person. A scientist takes cells from one person – a donor – to make the clone. The same cells could be used to make many copies of a donor, who would all be exactly alike.

So far, scientists have not made a clone from a human. There have only been animal clones.

So far...

Chapter 1
Death

DATELINE 26-5-2036

Doctor Connor's Office, Clones Inc.,
Los Angeles, California, 7:47 pm

I stared at Doctor Connor while I sat in his chair and put my feet up on his desk. He didn't care. He was dead.

He lay on a deep-pile carpet that had been white until he bled all over it. That wasn't his fault. Someone had put a bullet right through him. When that happened, all he could do was bleed. But if he'd died two metres to the left, he'd have missed the rug and fallen on the wooden floor. That would have made cleaning up much easier. Some guys don't care how much trouble they cause.

There were three other people in the room who weren't dead. But when I looked at Doctor Isadora Grey it was hard to be sure. She was as old, dry and wrinkled as an Egyptian mummy, but less of a looker. She had eyes like a bullfrog and a voice to match. She used it now. "Well?" she croaked.

I shrugged. "Shot through the heart at close range."

"Poor Doctor Connor," said the second person in the room. His name was Bristow. He was a skinny guy with a bad wig, who looked as if he was going to faint.

I ignored him. "No sign of a break-in," I said, "so Doctor Connor must have known his killer. Can I get a coffee here?"

"Brilliant!" This comment came from a big guy in a good suit. He was Head of Security at Clones Inc. His name was Harvey. He had a scar that ran right down his face from his right eye to his chin. He thought he was tough. He wasn't. The real tough guy was the one who gave him the scar. "Call yourself a Private Investigator?" he said with a sneer.

"Zak Taylor, P.I.," I grinned. "That's what it says on my badge. And the P.I. stands for Private Investigator."

"Yeah? Some investigator! Everything you just told us, we'd worked out for ourselves," Harvey said. He turned to Doctor Grey. "I told you we didn't need some dumb P.I. My men can handle this."

He'd wish he never said that. I was going to charge Clones Inc. an extra fifty bucks just for Harvey's "dumb P.I." crack. I stood up. "Well, if you don't need me ..."

"Sit down, Mister Taylor," snapped Doctor Grey. She had the sort of voice that expects to be obeyed. The sort of voice that teachers have – or hospital nurses and five star generals.

I sat down.

"You know why you're here," Doctor Grey went on. "Right now, Clones Inc. is in deep trouble. The public don't like clones. Judge Adam doesn't like clones, and he's head of the Supreme Court, so what he says counts. The President doesn't care about clones but he sure as hell likes votes so he's got to stay sweet with what people think. That's why we don't want the police here. We don't need anyone to know about this murder. If this gets messy, the scandal will close us down."

"I've got news for you." I pointed at Connor's body. "It's already messy."

"Not if we find who the killer is and hand him over to the police with all the evidence they need, tied up in a big pink ribbon," Doctor Grey said. "You tell us who the killer is – problem solved!"

I nodded. "OK. Let's start with the gun. It worries me. Why leave the gun at the crime scene? I suppose the killer did wipe it clean?"

Harvey gave me a nasty smile. "You suppose wrong. It's crawling with the killer's DNA."

I stared at him. "Then you have a suspect?"

Harvey's smile grew bigger. "You bet. In fact, we have thirty."

Chapter 2
Suspects

Doctor Connor's Office, 7:53 pm

I stared at Harvey for a second before the nickel dropped. "You're talking about clones, right?" I asked.

Harvey looked angry that I'd guessed right. But Doctor Grey smiled. "Well done, Mister Taylor. They told me you were good." She nodded. "Yes. Every human being's DNA is different. But every batch of clones is grown from cells from just one donor, so they all share that donor's DNA. The DNA on the gun matched that of the Cain clones grown by Doctor Connor."

"And there are thirty of these Cain clones?" I wanted to know.

"Correct. Mister Taylor, clones are our business. We make clones to work in high-risk jobs. Jobs like fire-fighting and working on oil rigs. Jobs that our health and safety experts tell us are too dangerous to be done by humans."

"I don't need a lecture on clones, Doc," I muttered.

Doctor Grey ignored me. "The clones we make are trained not to worry about their own safety," she went on. "And if one clone dies doing a dangerous task, the company just sends in another clone – there are plenty more. We speed up our results. Accelerated

Development Techniques mean a clone can be grown and trained in just three years."

"OK." I tipped my chair back and folded my hands behind my head. "The clones did it. So what do you need me for?"

"We want to know *which* of the clones did it, and why."

I grinned. "I get it. You can't let a killer clone out. It might kill again, and then it would be Clones Inc.'s fault. But you don't want to get rid of all thirty Cain clones. They're expensive. You need to prove that one clone is guilty. Then you can destroy it and hire the others out. No more worries."

Doctor Grey looked angry. "I wouldn't terminate any clone that had done nothing wrong."

"What's to stop you?" I said. "Clones have no human rights. They can't own property.

They *are* property. The clones you produce belong to your company. If they don't work hard, or if they break the law, the company has the right to terminate them."

"Mister Taylor, have you heard of genetic engineering? Clones are genetically engineered so that they *cannot* kill. If news gets out that one of our clones has killed, that would mean the end of this company! And with us out of the way, our rivals, Universal Clones, would get all the business – all our sales, all our profits."

I shrugged. "Things are tough all over," I grunted. When Doctor Grey said nothing, I went on, "OK. So if the clones' DNA is on the gun, at least one of them must have held it. Have you run GSR tests on the clones? If one of them fired the gun, there'll be gun powder traces on him."

"Of course." Harvey was annoyed. "All the clones tested negative. But the guy with the gun only had to wear a cover-all. There are plenty of those around."

"And the gun you found in this office *is* the one that killed Doctor Connor?"

Harvey stared at me, "Why wouldn't it be? It had been fired."

I shook my head. The man was an idiot. "Doctor Grey, I advise you to run a ballistics test. Check that the gun that was found in this office was the murder weapon."

"Do you think it wasn't?" Doctor Grey asked.

"No, I think it was. But that's just what I guess. An investigator deals in facts, not guesses. Now, let's see if we can narrow the list of suspects down a little. Do you have any reason to suspect one clone more than the others?"

Doctor Grey took her time before replying. Then she said, "Tell him, Bristow."

The skinny guy in the wig looked even more unhappy. His voice shook as he said, "Doctor Connor was doing experiments on the Cain batch."

This sounded interesting. "What was he trying to do?"

Bristow mumbled, "He was trying to make a clone that ... that could kill."

The front legs of my chair hit the carpet with a thud. "You don't say! Well, this is just a wild guess, but it looks to me as if he succeeded!"

Chapter 3
Killer

Doctor Connor's Office, 8:08 pm

"So, Doctor Connor was trying to make a killer clone." I leaned forward on the dead doctor's desk. "Does anyone want to tell me why?"

It was Doctor Grey who answered. "The army came to us." She shifted about in her chair. "They've been having trouble finding new men."

I nodded. "I guess people don't like the idea of being shot at. You can't blame them. A thing like that could ruin your whole day."

"Wise guy," muttered Harvey.

Doctor Grey frowned. "Very funny, Mister Taylor – but you are, in fact, correct. The army asked whether our clones could be soldiers. We told them that our clones have little fear of being killed. But we also explained that clones are made, and trained, not to be violent or aggressive. In short, not to kill."

"I can see that would be a big problem for a soldier," I said harshly. "I can guess the rest. You told Connor to make a clone that wasn't afraid of being killed, but was able to kill." I felt sick thinking about what Clones Inc. had done. "You guys slay me!" I said and shook my head. "You want clones to do all your dirty work and now you want them to die for you as well!"

Harvey gave me a nasty look. "What are you, Taylor? Some kind of lousy clone-lover?"

I shot to my feet, fists up. Harvey stepped forward with a snarl.

"That's enough!" Doctor Grey shouted. "Mister Taylor, do you want this job or not?"

I didn't. But if I didn't take it, maybe Doctor Grey would cut her losses and terminate all thirty Cain clones. Then again, if I didn't find the killer, she might do that anyway. So I'd better take the job and find out who killed Doctor Connor.

"All right," I said. "Bristow, do you know which of the clones Doctor Connor was experimenting on?"

He shook his head firmly. "No."

"Did the other clones know?"

Bristow gave a shrug. "I don't know. I can't even be sure that the changed clone knew himself."

I looked quickly at Doctor Connor's body. "I'm guessing he does now! So the other clones didn't know who the changed clone was – or at least, twenty-nine of them didn't. Or maybe they did know who it was. If so, do you think they'll tell me? This case stinks."

Harvey was still sore with me. "Did you think the killer would give himself up the minute you walked in here? Earn your money, big shot."

I took no notice. "I guess it's time I saw these clones for myself."

Chapter 4
Clones

Cain Clones' Recreation Room,
8:51 pm

I looked at the Cain clones. The Cain clones looked back at me. I don't suppose they were happy with what they saw. I knew for a fact I wasn't.

Clones give me the creeps. One clone's OK but there's something weird about a bunch of clones, all together. Thirty faces – all exactly the same – stared back at me. Spooky.

The Cain clones had short, stiff blond hair, tight lips and deep-set eyes that gave nothing away. Something about them looked familiar, but I couldn't work out what it was.

Maybe they'd been cloned from some TV celebrity. That happens a lot. If you have to make a lot of copies of a person, you may as well choose a donor who looks good. There's never a problem finding donors. So-called celebrities queue around the block to be cloned. If one of their fire-fighter clones rescues a puppy from a burning house, it's good for their image.

Of course, if one of their clones turns out to have committed murder, that's not such a great career move.

I was seeing the Cain clones in their rec room. I'd annoyed them already. I'd told them to turn the TV off. They'd been watching a football game. I was doing them a favour – it was a lousy game anyway. All football has been lousy since the top teams started using clones of their best players. Clones don't care if they win or not. But you can't have real people playing contact sports any more. Football is *dangerous*.

"Doctor Connor is dead," I told them. Shock tactics.

It didn't work. "Yeah, we heard," said one of the clones.

"Who told you?" I asked.

"Harvey," another one of them said.

So much for shock tactics. Thanks again, Harvey. "Hear how he died?" I asked. The clones looked at each other and shrugged. "Someone put a bullet through his heart."

"Must have been someone with real good aim," said the clone who'd spoken first. "To hit his heart, I mean. I didn't even know he had one." The other clones smirked.

"Gee, I didn't think you'd be so upset." I could do sarcasm, too. It's part of P.I. training.

"Why should we be upset?" asked another clone.

"So you didn't like Doctor Connor?" I said.

The clones looked at each other again. When one of them spoke, it was clear he was speaking for them all.

"We hated him."

Chapter 5
Motive

Cain Clones' Recreation Room,
8:56 pm

"You hated him?" I sat back in my chair. "Why? He was like a father to you. He gave you life."

"Some father," said the clone who was doing most of the talking. "Big deal. We never asked him to. It's a cruddy life anyway."

"That's right," another clone chipped in. "Connor was a typical Ook." 'Ook' is a rude word used by clones for non-cloned humans. Short for 'One Of a Kind.'

"Yeah," said another clone. "Ooks want us to do the dirty work for them, but they won't admit we're just as human as them."

I'd heard it all before, but I wanted to keep them talking. "Not all Ooks, as you call them, are anti-clone."

"Most are. Look at Judge Adam."

"Yeah. We haven't any human rights anyway. But if he had his way, he'd even take away the rights we haven't got!"

This was getting off the point. "So why was Connor a typical Ook?"

"He didn't think of us as people. He treated us like machines. He didn't care about us. Why should we care what happened to him?"

I gave him a grin. "What's your name?"

"Cain 14." The clone showed me his ID tattoo on the inside of his left wrist.

"Well, Cain 14 – did you murder Doctor Connor?"

All the clones leaned forward. All of them. Every last one stared me right in the eye. It was scary.

It was Cain 14 who did the talking. "The answer is no. You could ask every one of us the same question and you'd get the same answer. I didn't do it, so I know they didn't do it." The other clones nodded. "We're all the same."

"Not all of you." The sudden stillness told me that all the Cain clones knew what Doctor Connor had done. They knew one of them was not the same as the rest.

Cain 14 folded his arms. "I think you're through here, Mister Detective."

I said, "One of you murdered Doctor Connor. I'm going to find out who it was. You know what will happen to the guilty clone." No reply. They knew, all right.

I stood up and made for the door. When I got there, I turned. "By the way – who did Doctor Connor use to make you? Who was the donor?"

Cain 14 said, harshly, "Clones don't get told that."

"Was it Doctor Connor himself? Did he use his own cells?" I asked.

"Do we look like it was Doctor Connor?"

Fair point. The clones were blond and had blue eyes. Connor had been dark with grey eyes. Did they know who their real donor was? I stared at them until they started to fidget in their seats.

"Are you done?" I didn't see who had spoken. It didn't matter. They were all on edge. Good. Nervous people make mistakes.

I nodded. "For now." I wagged a finger at them. "Don't leave town."

I went out. I'd let them stew for a while. Then I'd see them again. And this time, no more Mister Nice Guy.

Chapter 6
Donor

Security Chief Harvey's Office,
9:26 pm

Harvey looked up as I came into his office.
"Find out anything?"

"Think I'd tell you if I had? Do you have
any coffee?"

Harvey had a coffee machine, but no
coffee. I gave him the glare of a coffee addict

who wasn't getting his coffee, and growled, "I need your computer."

Harvey gave me a dirty look but he moved away from his desk. I sat down in his chair and began to tap at the key-board.

Several minutes later, I had a print-out on Clones Inc. note paper. I waved it at Harvey. "I need thirty copies of this."

"What am I, an office boy?" Harvey growled but he was under orders to help me all he could. He got busy at the photo-copier.

While he was pressing buttons, I asked him, "Who was the original donor for the Cain clones?"

"How should I know?" Harvey was sulking. I waited. "He wouldn't tell me," Harvey said at last. "He wouldn't tell anyone. He always grinned when anyone asked him that. He seemed to think it was a big joke. Does it matter?"

"I don't know." I chewed my lip. "It might. They look kind of familiar. Like I've seen them some place before."

Harvey gave a shrug. "Maybe the donor came off some Z-list of TV celebs."

"Maybe. But in that case, what did Connor find so funny?"

The copier gave a final click and whirr, and Harvey took the finished copies from the out tray. He glanced at the top copy. Then he looked closer and his eyes bugged. He gave me an angry look. "Is this a joke?"

I shook my head. "Deadly serious."

Harvey tapped the papers with a finger like a banana. "But this is nonsense!"

I patted him on the cheek. "Don't sweat it, big guy. This 'nonsense' is going to catch us a killer."

Chapter 7
Test

Clones Inc. Teaching Room A,
9:48 pm

I'd come to see the Cain clones again. If they were pleased to see me, they hid it well.

They were sitting in a school-room. They must have been there many times before, learning to read, write and do maths. I could imagine thirty Cain clones kids sitting in this same room. I could almost hear their young voices chanting, "Once times two is two, two times two is four ..."

I gave the thirty identical faces a big friendly grin. "Anyone want to confess to Connor's murder and save me a lot of time? It's way past my bed-time and momma likes to tuck me in." Nothing. "Maybe it was an accident with the gun. Happens all the time. Tell me who did it. 'Fess up, and I'll do what I can to get the company to show mercy. What do you say?" Still nothing.

I sighed. "OK. Let's do this the hard way." I held up the papers. "Ever heard of offender profiling?" The clones gave each other worried looks. "There are thirty questions here. You will all answer every question as best as you can. You will not discuss the answers with each other." I gave out the papers and cheap pens with the Clones Inc. logo on the side.

The clones read the papers. They looked up. One said, "What sort of dumb questions are these?"

"I don't need you to like them. All I want is your answers," I said.

"But Question 3: Is your favourite type of ice-cream: a) Choc-choc Sundae, b) Taffy Chunx, or c) Strawberry Fool? We don't even *like* ice-cream! What on Earth is *any* answer to that going to tell you about who killed Doctor Connor?"

"It will tell me which of you is the changed clone. The questions are set by top experts to find out your deepest secrets. You can't know what you're really being asked unless you have the key to the test. You can't beat the test. If you try to cheat, that will show up in your profile. So there's no point trying." I checked my watch. "Don't forget to put your name and number at the top of the paper. You have fifteen minutes."

As they wrote (they all sucked the top of their pens while they were thinking), I watched the Cain clones. I still hadn't had a cup of coffee. This was making me feel very mean.

When the last clone had stopped writing, I said, "Time's up."

I collected the papers and started to look through them. Thirty pairs of eyes watched my every move. I glanced at most of the papers and put them at the bottom of the pile. But about half-way through, I stopped. I took one paper, looked at it very carefully, read every answer. The Cain clones leaned out of their chairs to try and see what I'd found.

I gave a short laugh and nodded. I made a great show of checking the number on the top of the paper. I nodded again.

I gave the Cain clones a crocodile smile. "Thank you, gentlemen. I have to confirm the results with a computer check. That's the rules. But there's really no need. I know who the killer is."

Chapter 8
Attempt

The Lobby, Clones Inc., 10:25 pm

After I left the Cain clones, I finally
tracked down a coffee machine. I put a coin
in and chose a latte. The machine poured out
the coffee but forgot about the cup, so I
ended up with my left shoe full of milk and
my right shoe full of espresso. Perfect.

Shortly after this, I was crossing the
entrance lobby on my way to Doctor Grey's
office when someone tried to kill me. A yucca

plant in a heavy pot came hurtling down
from a balcony several floors above.

Luckily, I was expecting it. Not a yucca plant – but an attempt on my life. I threw myself to one side and the plant hit the marble floor. Leaves, earth and pottery flew everywhere. Looking up, I saw a shadowy figure dart away from the rail of the third-floor balcony.

Harvey arrived, gun in hand, 'what-the-hell'-ing. I told him to lock down the building.

"Make sure nobody gets in or out," I ordered. "Then take a couple of men to the floor where the Cain clones live and do a head count."

"Why?" he asked. "There are thirty of them!"

It was a pity that someone had thrown the yucca plant, not Harvey, from the balcony. The yucca would have been a better Head of Security.

x

"I'm betting that there are twenty-nine right now," I told him. "Lock them in their rooms, put a guard on them, and search the building."

"For what?"

Was this guy for real? "For the clone that just tried to kill me!" I said.

****

Doctor Grey's Office, 10.40 pm

Harvey pushed our prisoner down into a chair – not too gently.

Doctor Grey raised an eyebrow. "You've got him?"

I explained about the attack. "Harvey's head count showed that Cain 27 was missing. We searched the building until we found him in a broom cupboard. He's the killer clone, all right. He put down Harvey and two of your boys – even though they were armed and he wasn't." Harvey rubbed his neck and glared at Cain 27. He'd been lucky. If I hadn't been there and put the clone in a strangle hold when I did, Doctor Grey would have been looking for a new Head of Security.

Doctor Grey looked at Cain 27 as if he was a bug under a microscope. "Why did you try to kill Mister Taylor?"

"He knew I was the changed clone." Cain 27's voice was low and hopeless. "I was scared. I was crazy. I didn't know what else to do."

"You should have sat tight and done nothing," I told him. "The test was a con. The questions were pointless. The results told me nothing. But I let you think they did. So you tried to kill me before I could tell anyone else you were the one that had been changed."

Cain 27 called me names that would have made a gangster blush.

"Did you find out what Doctor Connor had done to you?" I asked him. "Or did he tell you? Was that when you decided to kill him?"

The clone looked me right in the eye. "I tried to kill you. I'll plead guilty to attempted murder. But apart from that, you're way off base. I did not kill Doctor Connor!"

"Yeah? Says you ..." I broke off as the door of Doctor Grey's office burst open. A big man with white hair strode in. He was wearing a tuxedo and grinning like a Halloween lantern.

Doctor Grey sat back in her chair and glared at the newcomer. "That's all we need. Judge Adam!"

Chapter 9
Judge

Doctor Grey's Office, 10:51 pm

"Doctor Grey!" The head of the Supreme Court sounded as chummy as a daytime TV host. There was a smile on his face but none in his eyes.

The charm wasn't working on Doctor Grey. "What are you doing here?" she snapped.

"My civic duty." Judge Adam sat down and crossed his legs. "I hear you've failed to report a murder."

Doctor Grey told him that Clones Inc. was going to report a murder as soon as they were ready. While she was doing that, I scribbled a note and gave it to Harvey. He read it. Just for once he didn't ask stupid questions – he just gave me a nod and went out.

Judge Adam didn't even notice. "Don't give me that, Doctor," he said. "You have to report a murder right away. The police must be told at once. But you *didn't* tell them. You hired a low-life P.I. instead ..." He gave me a look of total dislike. "Because you knew that if it got out that one of your precious clones was a killer, you'd be in big trouble."

"You're right," I told him. "Doctor Connor's murder hasn't been reported. So I expect Doctor Grey would *love* to hear how you know about it – and how you know our chief suspect is a clone."

Doctor Grey's eyes flashed. "An excellent point, Mister Taylor." She gave Adam a cold stare. "How *did* you know?"

Judge Adam shrugged, and clicked his fingers. Doctor Connor's assistant, Bristow slid through the open door.

Doctor Grey gave him a look of disgust. "I thought we had a spy in the company. I should have known it was you! You must have run to Judge Adam as soon as you could. How much did he pay you?"

"That doesn't matter." Judge Adam batted the question away. He leaned forward and stared at Cain 27. "So this is the murderer."

"Maybe," I said. "He says he didn't do it."

"Of course he does." Adam stood up. "He's my prisoner now. I'll soon get at the truth." He leant across Doctor Grey's desk and his voice became cold and hard. "When I do, I'll make an example of him that will show every clone who's boss around here. And then I'll close down Clones Inc. – for good."

He turned to leave – and ran straight into me.

"What's the hurry?" I asked. I pointed at Cain 27. "Aren't you going to read him his rights?"

"He's a clone!" the Judge spat. "He doesn't have any rights!"

"No, he doesn't. Thanks to you. Clones have no rights, only numbers." I put my thumb and forefinger in my mouth, and gave a loud whistle. Harvey came back into the room – followed by six of the Cain clones. "Six of them, one of you," I told Judge Adam. I turned to the clones. "Hold him."

The clones grabbed Adam. They looked as if they were enjoying themselves. I couldn't blame them.

"Mister Taylor!" Doctor Grey's voice was harsh. "Do you have any idea what you're doing?"

"Just making sure Judge Adam co-operates," I told her. "He's going to take a DNA test. We'll need it as evidence when we charge him."

"Are you insane?" roared Adam. "Charge me with what?"

"Murder."

Chapter 10
Witness

Doctor Grey's Office, 11:07 pm

Doctor Grey sat at her desk and put her head in her hands. "Are you mad?"

"Hear me out," I told her. "Can you make up a DNA profile for this man?"

"Of course I can!"

"Then do it."

Doctor Grey stared at me for a moment. Then she said, "What the hell – I've nothing to lose!" She took a test kit from her desk.

Judge Adam went crazy. But the clones held him while Doctor Grey took a swab from the inside of his mouth. She put the swab in a plastic sample tube. Then she slotted the tube into a machine connected to her desk computer. Lights flashed in the machine and it began to hum.

I said, "While we're waiting for the results, let me tell you what I think happened. You can correct me if I'm wrong." Judge Adam glared at me. He was on his knees. He was panting, and his jacket was torn. There was hate in his eyes. I just wasn't making any friends today. "My guess is that Bristow found out that Connor had used Judge Adam's DNA to produce the Cain clones."

"What?" Doctor Grey sat up fast.

"Look at them together."

Doctor Grey looked from Adam to the face of one of the clones who was holding him – then back again. "My God, you're right. They *are* alike."

"I'm good at remembering faces – it's part of my training. As soon as I saw the Cains, I knew they made me think of someone. I just didn't know who. But when Judge Adam burst in here, I knew who it was at once."

"But – if you're right – how did Connor come to have Adam's DNA?"

"You have to give a DNA sample when you become a judge. That's the law. Somehow, Connor got hold of Adam's sample. He used it to make the Cain clones. That was what he found so funny when Harvey asked him who the donor was."

Doctor Grey's computer beeped. She checked the screen and nodded. "You're right. Judge Adam's DNA and that of the Cain clones are a perfect match."

I turned to Bristow. "You found out and told Adam."

Bristow was sweating. "I don't know what you mean."

I pointed at the Cain clones. "Do you want me to round up some more of these guys? You can tell them how come you tried to frame one of them for murder. I'm sure they'll be very understanding ..."

"All right!" Bristow started to talk, "I told Judge Adam about the Cain clones. And I let him into the building. I left him at the door of Doctor Connor's office. That's all I know."

I nodded, and tuned back to Adam. "You hate clones. You were furious that Connor had used your DNA. You demanded that he terminate the Cain clones. He said no. That's when you killed him."

Adam struggled to his feet. I told the Cains to let him up. They stood back.

"You're right," rasped Adam, "up to a point. I did go and see Connor. I would have told him to get rid of the monsters he had made from my DNA." The Cains growled. "But I didn't get the chance. When I arrived, Connor wasn't alone." Judge Adam pointed at Cain 27. "*He* was there. And *he* killed Doctor Connor! I saw him – I was a witness!"

Chapter 11
Verdict

Doctor Grey's Office and the Lobby,
Clones Inc., 11:14 pm

Cain 27 jumped up. "Liar!" His face was
dark with anger. "*He* was the killer! I found
him standing over Connor's body. He had the
gun in his hand. He'd have killed me, too, if I
hadn't got out of there real fast."

"So why didn't you tell anyone?" I asked.

"Are you kidding? My word against the Head of the Supreme Court? Who would you believe?"

"Exactly." Judge Adam was gloating. "Who would anyone believe? This *thing* would say anything to save his skin. But I'll see to it that he pays for his crime."

Cain 27 went for him. Adam must have been a fit guy when he was young, because his clone was *fast*. First he put Harvey down with a karate kick. Then he got his fingers around Adam's neck. I tried to drag him off and took a chop to the throat that made me lose interest for a while.

But Adam was a fighter. He broke the clone's strangle-hold, and made a run for it. Cain 27 followed.

"Taylor! Stop them!" That was Doctor Grey. Well, that was easy for her to say. She didn't have to tackle two desperate men.

Some days, I really earn my money. My throat still hurt but I set off after Adam and his clone.

They were headed for the lobby. There was no escape that way. There were armed guards on every door.

Adam saw them and headed for the stair-way. He was pretty fast, too, for an old guy.

The lobby went right up to the top of the Clones Inc. building – all ten floors. The stair-way ran up to the glass dome in the roof. There were balconies at every floor. Adam just kept going with the clone close behind him.

I set off after them. I was still groggy. My legs felt like lead.

I was half-way up when I saw them on the top balcony. They were fighting, grappling back and forth like wrestlers. They didn't say anything – just grunted as they fought.

At last, the clone backed Adam onto the balcony rail. Adam fell back over it, and dragged Cain 27 with him.

They were still trying to kill each other as they hit the ground.

Chapter 12
Case Closed

The Lobby, Clones Inc., Midnight

The bodies had been cleared away.

The police had turned up real fast when they heard Judge Adam was dead. They had taken over the building. Officers in cover-alls were taking pictures and looking for clues. Good luck to them.

The police had already talked to me.
They'd said I could go. They knew where to
find me if they needed me again

Harvey and Doctor Grey were talking in
low voices. Harvey was still limping.

I went over to them. Doctor Grey gave a bitter smile. "I suppose you expect me to thank you."

I shrugged. "I solved the case."

"Did you? So which of them did kill Doctor Connor? Was it Cain 27? Or Judge Adam?"

"We'll never know that. Does it matter? Maybe Cain 27 was the murderer because he hated Connor for creating him. Or maybe Adam was the murderer because he didn't like it that Connor used his DNA. Either way, it was really Connor's fault. He was the culprit. They're all dead, so what difference does it make? There'll be no trial. Everything is wrapped up nice and neat, just the way you wanted."

Doctor Grey shook her head. "The scandal will kill us."

"Sorry," I said. "Can't help you there. I'm in P.I., not P.R." I looked through the big windows, out across the dark city. My next case could be brewing out there. There might be excitement. There might be danger. There might even be coffee.

I turned at the door. "Oh – about my fee. Make the cheque out to Zak Taylor 7." Doctor Grey and Harvey stared at me. I enjoyed the look of shock on their faces. "Didn't the office tell you? I'm a clone myself." I nodded at what was left of the yucca plant and its pot. "After all – being a Private Investigator is a dangerous game!"

Glossary

Clones: Clones are an exact copy of one person, made from cells of that person. The same cells could be used to make many copies of that one person and they would all be exactly alike.

DNA: DNA is the code that holds information about the body. It controls such things as eye colour. DNA can be used as a 'genetic fingerprint' to identify criminals from bits of skin or strands of hair at the scene of a crime. Scientists check the DNA in the skin or hair to see whose it is.

Genetic Engineering: In genetic engineering (also known as genetic modification) DNA is changed to 'improve' a plant or animal. For instance, with genetic engineering, scientists can breed plants that produce more food or resist disease. They are called GM plants or crops. Environmental groups are very concerned about the introduction of GM foods into the human food chain.

Accelerated Development Techniques: In the future it may be possible to make a person's body and mind grow faster than normal. Scientists who are looking for ways to do this call them Accelerated Development Techniques.

GSR (Gun Shot Residue) tests: When a gun fires, it throws out a fine dust of the heavy elements barium, lead and antimony. Forensic scientists can test someone's hands, arms and face to see if any of that dust is on them. Then they will know if that person has fired the gun.

Ballistics: Ballistics is the science of studying bullets and bullet impacts. A ballistics expert can look at a bullet taken from a victim to find out which gun fired the fatal shot.

Donors: The people who give their cells to scientists for experiments are called donors.

Offender Profiling: This is a way in which detectives can build up a 'picture' of an unknown person by putting together all the information they have about the person. They'll use the information to make a guess about how that person might look, think and behave.

DNA Profile: A 'reference sample' of a person's DNA is taken by collecting cells from inside the mouth with a swab. This sample is then analysed to find the person's DNA profile, or 'genetic fingerprint'.

Private Investigation (P.I.): Private Investigators don't work for a police department. They are detectives who work for anyone and charge a fee for their services.

Public Relations (P.R.): People who work in public relations are sometimes called 'spin doctors'. It's their job to pass on news about their company or their government. Of course, they will try and make that news look good.

A swab: A swab is like a cotton bud. It is used to take samples of saliva from a person's mouth.

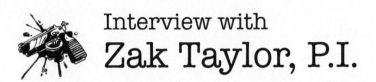

Interview with
Zak Taylor, P.I.

Which 3 words would people use to describe you?

Cool. Sarcastic. Broke.

What are the best things about being a P.I.?

Working your own hours. Bringing in the bad guys. Baffling the cops.

And the worst?

The hours are lousy. Not enough sleep. Being broke.

Are there any cases you've not solved?

Yeah – who was Jack the Ripper? Who took the cookie from the cookie jar? Otherwise, no.

Has anyone ever tried to kill you (apart from the Killer Clone!)?

Happens all the time. I'm Zak Taylor 7. There used to be 15 of us. Now there are only 8. Things are tough all over.

What is the secret to solving a crime?

Keep asking questions. Pay attention to the answers. Trust nobody.

Barrington Stoke would like to thank all its readers for commenting on the manuscript before publication and in particular:

Rob Barron

Robert Brooks

Tyler Bumpass

Grant Butler

Lucy Butler

Andrew Campbell

Mary Campbell

Jade Cheneau

Mark Clark

Ronnie Forsythe

Will French

Tom Goodenough

Paul Montgomery

Nick Mould

Simon Joseph Nicholls

Liam Parham

Morag Patterson

Matty Pratley

Mark Smallwood

Sarah-Jayne Wilkinson

GRACEMOUNT HIGH SCHOOL

LIBRARY

Become a Consultant!

Would you like to give us feedback on our titles before they are published? Contact us at the email address below – we'd love to hear from you!

info@barringtonstoke.co.uk
www.barringtonstoke.co.uk